This is the story of

ALISON HUBBLE

who went to bed single...

Allan Ahlberg Bruce Ingman

PUFFIN

And woke up double.

Woke up with a twin
In her single bed.
"Who are you?" "Who are you?"
She said, she said.

Then her dad came in.

"Good grief! Ye gods!"
Mr Hubble groaned
As he gazed at the sight
Of Alison cloned.

"I can't believe it
It's hardly fair
One daughter's enough
We don't need a pair!"

Then Mrs Hubble came in.

"Oh, Alison, Alison!"
Cried her mother.
"You always said
You wanted a brother.

"I'm quite overcome
Your gran'll go wild
We don't expect this
From an only child."

After that Alison had a word (or two).

But what to wear?

said Alison Hubble.

By and by Alison went to school
with a letter for the teacher.

Dear Mrs Mott,
I thought I ought to write a note about
our Alison who doubled in the night.
Her father and I were powerless to
prevent what can only be described
as this singular event. We're sorry
indeed to put you to this trouble.
  Yours sincerely,
    Maureen Hubble
P.S. Her extra dinner money is enclosed.

Well, at first it was fun –
Lots of laughs –
And a queue formed at playtime
For her autographs.

Presently, however, there was a spot of bother.

Her friends said, "But, Alison,
Which one's really you?
Come on, we're flummoxed
Give us a clue."

Well, I'm me!

said Alison.

And I'm me, too.

No you're not— what rubbish.

I'm more me than you.

Later, while children were getting ready for games . . .

The cloakroom was crowded
But got crowded even more
When – all of a sudden –

There was Alison times four!

She had doubled again
In seconds flat
Like magical rabbits
From a conjuror's hat.

Her friends were delighted
And concerned for her fate.
"Poor Alison!" they sympathized
And, "This is great!"

They argued in the football match
Which team she should be in.
"With Alison in goal
We'd be bound to win."

Then it was hometime.

When Alison came through the door
And kept on coming
Her father put his glasses on
And starting drumming
With his fingers on the table
And then he said, "Ye gods!
It was bad enough before –
Now we've got quads!"

Alison, meanwhile, was feeling hungry.

Cheese for me!

I'd like ham!

Boiled egg and salad, please!

Bread and jam!

Then she went outside
and upstairs too
And sat in the kitchen
and sat on the loo,
Did the washing up
And some of the drying . . .

Ran into the garden
And knocked herself flying.

At eight o'clock Alison went to bed.

She tiptoed on the landing
Giving herself a scare
As she whispered in the darkness,
"Alison, you still there?"

And before she went to sleep
Each one of her stared at the ceiling
With a puzzled look on her face
And a curious quadruple feeling.

When morning came, Mrs Hubble
Called to her husband, "Ted!
Wake up, come on, go and count her
I can't bear to look," she said.

So Alison's father arose
And peered anxiously in at each door.
"There's two in here," he reported.
"And two in the bath makes four."

"And two in the kitchen!" cried Alison.
"And two on the stairs makes ten."
(Maths wasn't her strongest subject.)
"I think I've doubled again."

Later, she had her breakfast and went . . .

off   and off   and off   an

ff 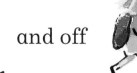 and off  and off  and off and off to school.

Where a crowd was waiting
At the playground gate
With a noisy welcome,
"Two – four – six – eight!"

A reporter was there
From the local press.
"Who's Alison Hubble?"
And the crowd said,

"Guess!"

The photographer with him
Lined Alison up
Like a football team
That had won the cup.

Eventually, Alison reached her classroom
and the teacher called the register . . .

Extra books were needed
Extra chairs and tables.
Said Mrs Mott (all muddled up)
"What you girls need are labels!"

After school, Alison came home to find her dad in his best suit . . .

And her mum, looking brave
With a cup of tea
Being interviewed for the BBC
While the crowd in the street
Went, "Oooh!" and "Aaah!"
"Here's Alison, et cetera."

IT'S NOT FAIR!

BBC

There were TV cameras
A TV van
Microphones, cables
and Alison's gran . . .

Who was complaining about
the unfairness of it all.

But Alison by now
Had complaints of her own.
"I'm fed up with crowds
I want to be alone."

She refused to be filmed
For the News at Ten
Stamped up to her room . . .

And doubled again.

"Oh, no!" said her mum
"What a tragedy!
It'll take us two hours
to cook her tea."

"You're right," said her dad
"It's rotten luck
We'll have to do the shopping
with a three-ton truck."

Alison, however, cheered up when
she went into the garden.

Yes, out on the lawn
Stood a great big tent
With sleeping bags too
Which the council had lent.

Yet even then
There were certain snags

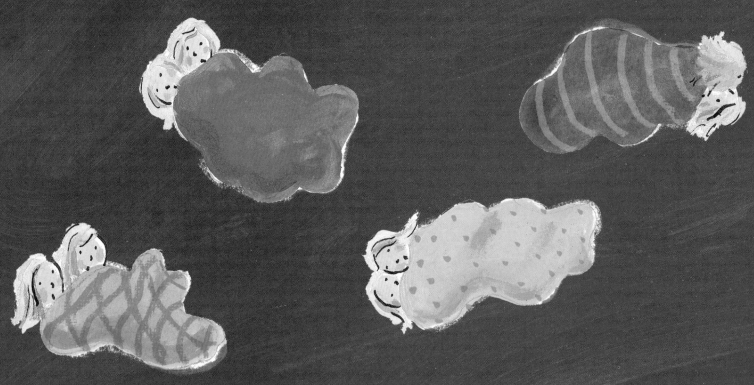

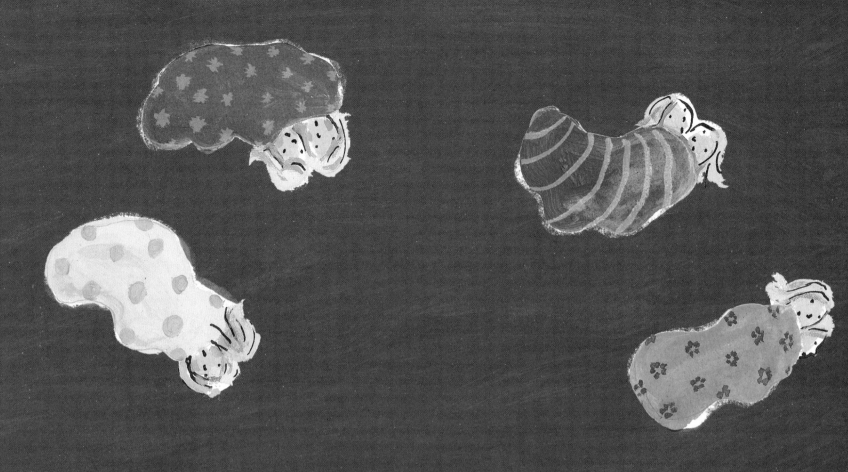

When she doubled that night
And got stuck in the bags!

In case you've lost count, there were now thirty-two of her.

Well, Alison's fame continued to spread.

SHE'S ONE IN A MILLION!

. . . the papers said.

Various professors and experts also took an interest in her.

They studied her tongues
And tapped her knees
And talked of split personalities.

And they wondered where
The world was heading
And whether or not
They could stop her spreading.

They are wondering yet
If you care to know
For the numbers of Alison
continue to grow.

She's lately reached
A huge amount
Though how many's uncertain . . .

They've all lost count.

Meanwhile Alison . . .

Who has, so to speak
Grown out of her tent
Is presently living
In Stoke-on-Trent.

ALL OF

The End
(not)